Twisted Tales

of

South Devon

by Jo Harthan

Twisted Tales of South Devon.

Illustrations, Artwork and Photographs: Joan C. Harthan

ISBN-13: 978-1976087820
ISBN-10: 1976087821

FRONT COVER - Photograph of skeleton in the crow's nest of The Golden Hind at Brixham, © **Jo Harthan 2017**

Contents

Wooden sculpture leaning seaward as if on the prow of an ancient ship. Located above St. Mary's Bay, near Brixham.

The Golden Hind at Brixham

This full-sized replica of The Golden Hind is permanently moored in Brixham harbour.

Dropping down from Berry Head, South West Coast walkers are treated to one of the most picturesque towns on the South Devon coast. Brixham is one of the best kept secrets of this coastline, often over-looked because of its close proximity to Torquay and Paignton.

It has a long and fascinating history. In the past, there were two separate communities here — Cowtown was the area on top of the hill where the farmers lived, and Fishtown was the harbour area where the fishermen lived. These areas are still celebrated today in the annual Cowtown Carnival.

The town also hosts a Pirates' Festival every May. Advertised as *'an annual gathering of the world's most infamous pirates and lowly scallywags',* the festival attracts revellers from all over the globe.

No surprise then to find, moored in the harbour alongside working trawlers, a full-sized replica of one of the most iconic ships of the piracy period. It is, of course, The Golden Hind — the Tudor Galleon made famous by Sir Francis Drake.

As well as plundering the Spanish galleons to line the coffers of Queen Elizabeth I, 'El Draco' or 'The Dragon' as Drake was known, was also instrumental in defending the realm against the invading Spanish Armada in 1588.

Indeed, the South Devon coastline has always been a target for invading armies. Even in modern times, its shores are littered with military units and defensive structures, all of which bear testimony to human folly — and remind us that the greed for power and territory are as prevalent in the human psyche today as they ever were. And, of course, the cruelty and lack of empathy that so often drives the greed, are the very traits that give the dark side of humanity its strength. But, to be fair, if it were not for such abhorrent human characteristics, I would not have anything to write about.

Which brings me to the photograph on the cover of this book. It was the skeleton, standing in the crow's nest of the rigging of The Golden Hind, that gave me the idea for another sort of invasion — the one portrayed in my story 'Tiger's Revenge' whose setting is Torcross and Plymouth. The story is based on the actual WWII rehearsals for the D-Day landings and reminds me that, whether we are invading or defending, perpetrator or victim, our life is a disposable asset for those who hold power over us.

FOREWORD

First let me apologise to all those Devonians who may take offence at my lumping all the southern areas of the county together. It was a necessary evil to avoid the title of my book being: *Twisted Tales of South and East Devon, including the English Riviera.* I'm sure you will agree that, whatever we call it, it is a beautiful part of our glorious English countryside.

All the tales in this collection were written, or inspired, whilst walking the South Devon stretch of the South West Coast Path. As I had set out on this path almost ten years earlier, it seemed prudent to get a move on and so I walked the entire South Devon coastline, from Plymouth to Seaton, in the summer of 2017. According to the online Distance Calculator, this stretch is 123.3 miles, though with all the diversions inland to avoid landslips or private property, the distance I walked was undoubtedly greater than that. The English weather, of course, never disappoints, and threw everything it had at me, from torrential rain storms to a blistering heat-wave. I feel rather lucky to have survived it relatively unscathed.

The end of the path is now fast approaching, (as I write this book, I only have another forty miles of the six hundred and thirty miles left to walk), and I am beginning to feel a little sad. This project has been a part of my life for such a long time and I'm not sure yet what will replace it. Perhaps when I reach Poole, I will simply turn around and walk all the way back in the opposite direction.

But . . . to the tales in this collection. Much of this coastline has a long history in the defence of our country, evidenced by a proliferation of old disused batteries that are scattered along the coastline. I could not ignore this important part of our heritage and, during my research for some of the stories, I learned a great deal about the politics and the sacrifices made in both the world wars. My generation were never taught modern history at school and so, what little I knew before this, was from commemoration events and the poetry of Owen and Sassoon, which I studied for English Literature as a sixteen-year old.

As is usual in my Twisted Tales series, the stories in this collection are a mixture of fact and fiction. The places are factual and provide the backdrop to the stories. The people, on the other hand, are fictitious, though some of the situations they find themselves in are based on true accounts.

The tales begin in an old disused coastguard look-out up on Revelstoke Drive, not too far from Plymouth. After evicting the sheep that were sheltering from the blistering hot sun, I spent a long time inside this one-roomed building, wondering what it would be like to live here. It was such an evocative place and, being perched high on the cliff, it had wonderful views of the coastline in both directions. On looking westward, I could see Great Mewstone rising up out of the water like a natural pyramid. It is actually an island but sadly is out of bounds to tourists and walkers as it is now a bird sanctuary. In the past, it has hosted a prison and a private home as well as having been a refuge for local smugglers. Its most infamous resident was Sam Wakeman who avoided transportation to Australia in favour of the cheaper option of transportation to the Mewstone, where he was interned for seven years. When his term of imprisonment was at an end, he voluntarily remained on the island, paying his rent by supplying rabbits for the Manor House table. So this area, with the history of the Mewstone in my thoughts, was the perfect place for a man, down on his luck, to hide away from the world. What happens to him at the end of my story is probably a reflection on the state of the path in some areas of South Devon! See the *Afterword* for more information on this.

Bolt Tail is mentioned in passing in 'Beware of the Rocks' but it is worth giving a little more detail here as its geology and pre-history helped forge my story. It lies just to the west of Soar Mill Cove and flint tools have been discovered here, dating from 6000BC. Today, the main archaeological monument is a late Iron Age promontory fort, giving evidence that this coastline has always been important in the defence of our country. This long history, along with legends of Celtic Shamanism and the strange rock formations that are to be found on the stretch of coast between here and Bolt Head, were the inspiration for my tale of rocks that come alive — either of their own volition or as a result of earth tremors. That's something you will have to decide for yourself.

Finally, as a child I was passionate about those cone-shaped bags of sweets called 'Lucky Bags'. The excitement of not knowing what I was going to find inside kept me spending my pocket money on them for years. And my tales are a little bit like that — setting out on each day's walk, I never knew what I was going to find. Like those bags, this is a 'Lucky Bag of Tales' — a mixture of gruesome murder, ghostly tales, sentient landscapes and wartime dramas. Though unlike the sweetie bags of my childhood, I do hope the contents here don't disappoint.

At the end of each story you will find information and explanations about the origins of the tales being told. These have been added for interest and background information.

It only remains for me to wish you the best of luck as you journey with my characters along this historic coastline. Perhaps my tales will entice you to walk at least some sections of the South West Coast Path yourself. If they do, I suggest that you stay vigilant, for if you encounter any strange occurrences, they may be a prelude to something far more sinister.

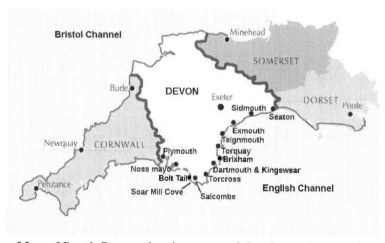

Map of South Devon showing some of the places that are the settings for this collection of Twisted Tales.

Twisted Tales

of

South Devon

Body in the Bracken

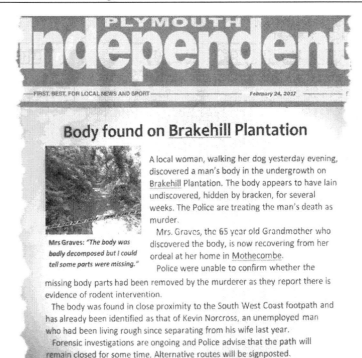

PLYMOUTH Independent

FIRST, BEST, FOR LOCAL NEWS AND SPORT — February 24, 2017

Body found on Brakehill Plantation

A local woman, walking her dog yesterday evening, discovered a man's body in the undergrowth on Brakehill Plantation. The body appears to have lain undiscovered, hidden by bracken, for several weeks. The Police are treating the man's death as murder.

Mrs Graves, the 65 year old Grandmother who discovered the body, is now recovering from her ordeal at her home in Mothecombe.

Mrs Graves: "The body was badly decomposed but I could tell some parts were missing."

Police were unable to confirm whether the missing body parts had been removed by the murderer as they report there is evidence of rodent intervention.

The body was found in close proximity to the South West Coast footpath and has already been identified as that of Kevin Norcross, an unemployed man who had been living rough since separating from his wife last year.

Forensic investigations are ongoing and Police advise that the path will remain closed for some time. Alternative routes will be signposted.

Kevin was sitting on the cold flag floor, head in hands. A chilly sea breeze was being funnelled through a hole where once there had been a window and it was biting through his t-shirt.

"Come on," he spoke out loud even though there was no one to hear, "you can do this."

He lifted his head and looked around. At least the roof and walls were in good condition, no problem there. The doorway was landward-side and sheltered from the worst of the weather but he would have to fix up a door to stop the sheep coming in.

~ 13 ~

He had seen the abandoned coastguard lookout last year when he'd been walking along the old Revelstoke Drive. Had even climbed up to it and wondered what it must have been like to be holed up here on a winter's night, scanning the open waters for smugglers or drug traffickers. He didn't know then that it would be his next home.

Or that he was about to lose his job — sacked the following week for settling an argument with his fists instead of his tongue. And now he had lost his wife. He had nothing else to lose. He told himself it was what he deserved. He had been the guilty party in both cases — too quick tempered at work and too many extra-marital affairs at home. Not that anyone would call them affairs, they were usually just one-night stands, two at the most. He wondered now if he should have stayed and weathered the storm with his wife. After all, where had she been sneaking off to when the kids were at school? She probably had her bit on the side as well. When he'd challenged her about it, she made some feeble excuse about a long-lost cousin suddenly getting in touch, wanting to catch up and reminisce about their childhood.

"Must have been a very eventful childhood," he said, "you've been seeing this 'cousin' three times a week for a month."

She answered by telling him to do the decent thing and leave. Clearly she had plans of her own. Truth was, he'd had enough and so he walked out, leaving her with the kids. He didn't think any of them would miss him.

And this is where it had landed him — living on a cliff in a one room hovel that smelled of sheep urine. On the plus side, there was a fireplace and a working chimney so at least he would be warm. Cooking could be done over the fire in an iron pot he had bought from a charity shop in Plymouth, along with a mug and a plate and a few pieces of old cutlery.

He would rest up here a while, lie low, sort himself out. No one need know. He didn't want visitors. He certainly didn't want his wife coming around demanding maintenance. She had got the house and all their savings — what more did she want? He'd left with nothing. One blessing was that his dole money was paid straight into his bank account so there was no need to contact the authorities who would, he suspected, have made a noose for him out of their red tape.

The first two weeks in his new home were back-breaking — doing the work of three men to make the place right. He begged, stole and borrowed whatever he could. One of the cottages in Mothecombe was being renovated and the builder said he was welcome to take whatever he wanted from the skip — an old door, a couple of almost-new PVC windows and scraps of wood to pack around them to make them fit. One of the lads even gave him two bags of sand and cement, telling him not to tell the gaffer. Soon it felt like home, albeit just one small room with a makeshift bed along one side, made from blankets and a camping mattress that he had managed to scrounge from his brother. He felt like a boy again, camping out, living rough. A simple life was just what he needed to get his head back in gear. No hassle, no one to bother him. If the landowner turned up with a gun and a few expletives, he would move on. But until then he would make the most of things and enjoy the solitude.

He spent his days walking along the cliffs or through Brakehill Plantation. Unemployment benefit didn't stretch very far, so he couldn't afford much meat and he had never been one for vegetables, so he spent every Friday catching rabbits in Passage Wood. Rabbit stew had never tasted so good, especially with the few carrots and onions he always managed to stuff inside his jacket whenever he went to Tesco's. Unfortunately, bottles of booze were more difficult to hide and so he usually had to buy his indispensable weekly ration.

Getting water had been a problem. He couldn't afford bottled so a friend had lent him the water carrier he used for his caravan, which he filled in the toilets at the pubs in Noss Mayo or Mothecombe. It was hard work pulling it up onto the cliffs, but if he could manage a full load it would last him more than a week.

He had been in his make-shift accommodation for two months when he met Maxine. She was next in line signing on at Plymouth Job Centre and had turned to him with the sweetest smile, offering him a mint humbug. They got talking. She said her boyfriend had let her down, disappeared without a word. The doctor had put her on anti-depressants to help her cope with the prospect of endless lonely nights. She looked sad, eyes glazing over as though she was about to cry. He confided that he was going through the same thing, said his wife had left him for someone else. He didn't feel good about himself when he lied but it had become so much of a habit he hardly noticed it anymore. Maxine was full of sympathy and seemed to forget her own troubles, said that somehow it was worse for a man because women were more used to taking care of themselves. He reached out and squeezed her hand in gratitude and suggested they go for a coffee.

Usual dole rigmarole finished, they wandered over to Cafe Kiss on North Street and sat on a cosy leather settee for two. The smell of food was intoxicating and so they ordered two burgers with coffee. She insisted on paying, said she had just got lucky on a scratch card. Despite her depression, she was funny and flirtatious, all the things he found irresistible. And she had a car — an old Fiat Panda that groaned going up hills and rattled going down them.

He could never remember whose idea it had been — they seemed to have a weird sort of telepathic connection, but their next stop after Cafe Kiss was up on Jenny Cliff exploring the powerful animal lust that was at work between them. She said he was everything she had ever wanted in a man; powerful, rugged, intense. She was the healing touch that his ego needed to recover from the verbal abuse, and plates of hot food, that his wife had been throwing at him for years.

Jenny Cliff continued to be their rendezvous on signing-on days, but she lived in Plymouth and didn't mind driving, so most days they would meet up on his side of the River Yealm. On sunny days they would find a sheltered spot in fields around Noss Mayo or go to what they began to call their trysting-tree on Brakehill Plantation — a huge beech that slithered up above the canopy, its base hidden from the path by bracken and wild garlic. Like love struck teenagers they carved a huge heart into the trunk and put their initials inside, speared by Cupid's arrow.

As Summer turned to Autumn and the days began to chill, their rendezvous became his place on Revelstoke Drive. They would lie together on a thick blanket spread out over the flag floor in front of an open fire, drinking cheap cider and laughing in between bouts of taking whatever they could from each other's bodies. It was raw and passionate with a primacy that took over his thoughts and his life. He could think of nothing else but the feel of her soft flesh and the smell of their love-making. But as Winter closed in, and the frost began to bite, he started to tire of his bachelor pad. This was no place to spend cold winter months and so he asked about going to her place — perhaps moving in together. He expected her to be pleased but she dismissed the idea without explanation.

"No," was all she said. And she sounded angry, which confounded him. They had a good thing going and he thought they were solid.

The following day she was back to her sweet, smiling self and whispered, during a long, lusty kiss, "All in good time lover, all in good time."

He should have known it would end badly — relationships like that always do.

*   *   *

Christmastime arrived and brought with it a deep melancholia that he found hard to handle. He missed the kids and felt guilty at not being able to buy them good presents — though the week before Christmas he had sacrificed his usual Friday-night pints in The Swan at Noss Mayo and got Jack a toy car and Lucy some clips and ribbons for her hair. He had gone round to the house with them but his wife wouldn't let him in. She said he'd frighten the children with his dirty appearance and shaggy hair. She promised to give the gifts to them but he knew his wife too well — they were probably in the bin before he reached the end of the path.

To cheer him up, Maxine said she had a big surprise for him and to meet her at their trysting-tree between eleven and midnight on Christmas Eve. He had been putting aside a pound or two from his dole money for a few weeks, so he went and bought her a small bottle of Gucci Guilty, recommended by the sales girl who described it as spicy with musky undertones. That was definitely the one for Maxine. He saw it as an investment in his future — if she hadn't yet decided to let him move in with her, perhaps this would persuade her.

*   *   *

Christmas Eve was cold and cloudless, the ground covered in frost that glittered in a full moon, risen high in the sky. There was Christmas magic in the air — a magic he hadn't felt since he was a boy. Pulling his jacket closer around him, he hurried on over the steep wooded slopes, stepping over fallen beech trees broken by the winter storms. He came at last to their trysting-tree and sat on his haunches on the ground with his back to the tree, hoping to get a little shelter from the wind. There were dark shadows everywhere and the wind was making branches groan and leaves rustle.

At last he heard her approaching and raised himself to his feet. He peered through the trees but could not see her. He called her name. No answer. Then he heard it — a shrill scream for help, a woman's scream. Maxine's scream. He blundered through the thick undergrowth in the direction of the sound. The banking was steep and he was breathing heavily, slipping and sliding on the frozen bracken. And then he saw her. She was hanging by the neck from an oak tree, her face blue and frozen in the moonlight. She was wearing the thin voile dress that she'd so often teased him with — always naked underneath. He could see the soft roundness of her bare breasts and the dark shadow of pubic hair. He rushed over, supporting her on his shoulders to take the weight off her neck and reached up to untie the rope that was cutting into her throat. She groaned as he gently laid her on the ground. Taking off his jacket, he wrapped it around her, holding her close.

"Why?" he said, "Why have you done this?"

She tried to raise her head, "I didn't," she said, "It was him."

"Who?" he demanded, "Who did this?"

"I did," a voice behind him made him jump to his feet. He knew as soon as he saw the man that a fight was not an option — he was over seven feet tall with hands that looked like they could tear a man to pieces.

"I don't want any trouble," Kevin said, "just let me help her and we'll say no more about it."

The man took a step towards him. The situation had an air of unreality that Kevin was having trouble shaking off. Something wasn't right but he didn't know what, couldn't quite figure it out.

"What you been doin' wi' my girl?" the man asked, towering over Kevin like a huge bear.

"I'm sorry," Kevin shouted, "I didn't know she had a boyfriend. She never said."

"She never does pal. But that doesn't let you off the hook."

"Just let me help her," Kevin pleaded, "You've half killed her."

"She doesn't need your help," he said, "and you're next pal."

Kevin turned to run. He didn't owe Maxine anything and if this was the sort of fella she usually hung out with, he'd best leave her to it. He hadn't got far when a huge hand landed on his shoulder and pulled him backwards, lifting him off his feet before smashing him onto the ground.

"I'm really sorry," Kevin gasped. The side of his face was being pressed into a pile of frozen leaves, "I would never have gone with her if I'd known."

Surprisingly that seemed to appease the man and he pulled Kevin up into a sitting position. A look of great sadness came over his face. Taking his enormous form, he slumped down on the ground beside Kevin.

"She's always doing this to me," he said, "And it really hurts man, you know, when your woman is out there with other men and you're at home looking after the kids."

"Kids?" Kevin was startled, "she never mentioned she had kids."

"Didn't she?" the man replied, "would it have made any difference?"

Kevin shrugged, "Dunno mate."

"Was she any good?" The man asked.

Kevin wasn't sure what to say; he was anxious not to jeopardise this newly created camaraderie.

"She was okay," he said at last.

His words seemed to cause a rustling in the wood and soon Maxine's lithe body was sliding and swaying through the undergrowth towards them. She was moving like a snake, head raised from the ground, arms and legs propelling her forwards. Even in shock, Kevin couldn't help thinking he had never seen anything so grotesque, nor so frightening.

"So," she said as she reached them, seemingly no worse for wear, "I was okay was I?"

This wasn't good. Something was seriously out of kilter and he hadn't a clue what was going on. The last conversation he had with his wife suddenly began to replay in his head.

'You'll get your come-up-ence,' she had said to him, 'your sort always do.'

He pushed the thought aside and turned all his attention to Maxine,

"Are you alright?" he asked feebly, knowing how ridiculous his words must sound. She laughed.

"Got a bit of a sore throat," she said, "but that's nothing to what you're going to have."

"But he tried to kill you Maxine."

She laughed again, this time more loudly, "No he didn't," she said, "we were just playing. We like to play games. I thought you did too."

"Not those sort of games Maxine."

"That's a shame," she said, leaning her head forward and kissing his lips in the way that was usually a prelude to sex, "because you're coming to live with us. Let's call it a mutually beneficial Christmas present. You're our new toy. We'll have such fun together, the three of us."

He felt a sharp pain in his side and on looking down, saw she was holding a hypodermic.

His world faded into black and was gone.

*   *   *

Kevin woke some hours later with a creeping sense of horror. He was lying on his back in a dark room, half naked and cold. Judging from the smell of mould and damp, he guessed it must be a cellar. Candles had been left burning, casting dark shadows that were moving and morphing into dreadful apparitions, mirroring the monsters in his mind. His hands were free but there were metal chains around his ankles, bolted to the floor, keeping him prisoner. With great effort he got himself into a sitting position, slumping back against the wall for support. The flickering candlelight reminded him of the lusty, sweaty nights with Maxine, lying on blankets in front of the open fire. Memories that now filled him with horror.

As his eyes became more accustomed to the gloom, he saw there were photographs stuck on the wall beside him. The largest one was a photograph of his wife — a photograph he had taken on their honeymoon ten years earlier. And there were others, all of her. One taken by him at a friend's wedding, one with the kids in Anglesey on a camping holiday. The one at the top was more recent. Her hair was clipped up — the way she was wearing it when he had called with the kids' presents. Her smile was wide and surprised, as if she had just been given some exciting news.

He reached up to touch her smiling face, remorse washing over him in a baptism of regret. She hadn't deserved what he'd put her through. She was a good mother and a good wife, and if he got out of here he would make amends, try and win her back. The sound of a door opening interrupted his thoughts, followed by heavy footsteps lumbering down the stone steps. It was the man, reeking of cooked sprouts and beer.

"A very merry Christmas," he said as he handed Kevin a bowl of cold turkey, before settling himself onto an old packing case. "Under orders to watch you eat it. Got to keep your strength up. Besides Mrs don't want you breaking her crockery and doing yourself a mischief."

"Why are you doing this to me?" Kevin asked.

The answer he got was cruel and scornful and tore away any hope he had of escaping whatever they had in store for him.

"You brought it on yourself pal. You've been a bad boy and now it's payback time."

*   *   *

It turned out, payback time wasn't quite as soon as Kevin was expecting. The candles burned out and weren't replaced but the man brought food and water, and one day a thick blanket that smelled of the forest. He was grateful for that, at least it staved off the misery of being cold and gave some protection against the stone floor. It also gave him hope that they were only trying to frighten him. Well, they had succeeded in doing that. There was no daylight in the cellar and there was nothing to tell if it was day or night. He counted off the days by the man's visits, which were always signalled by the door at the top of the stone steps opening and torchlight flooding in. He assumed this only happened once a day as the hours in between seemed to last a lifetime. On what he counted as the sixth day, instead of bringing food, the man brought news of his fate.

"Time to play," he growled, unlocking the chains and yanking Kevin to his feet. Half-carrying and half-dragging, he hauled Kevin up the steps and took him to where Maxine was waiting. She was wearing the long red dress that she had worn the last time they'd had sex. It was silk and was flowing, blood-like, onto a canvas of stark, white walls. Cheap linoleum, with a crazy pattern of triangles in blue, yellow and red, covered the floor. Kevin saw the whole scene with frightening clarity. It was like a picture painted too brightly; a hellish hallucination on a bad trip. He could

~ 25 ~

see a selection of tools hanging from butcher's hooks in the corner — large scissors, a hammer, a saw, various sizes of pliers and screwdrivers, something that looked like a calliper. In the middle of the room was a large, rectangular metal table. He struggled to pull free of the man, using all that remained of his strength to shout and scream for help. But it was useless. Maxine was laughing as her boyfriend hauled Kevin onto the table, tying his arms and legs securely at each corner.

When playtime started, he screamed for mercy, begging Maxine to remember the good times they'd had together, pleading with her to stop. But his panic only seemed to deepen her enjoyment. Her face glowed with the excitement of it all.

It was the saw that inflicted the worst pain and blood soon covered the table on which he lay. It felt warm on his back, giving him a bizarre sort of comfort. But all too soon it dripped away onto the floor leaving him colder than before. Eventually, the pain was so bad it robbed him of all sound. There was no coming back from this. This was the end.

As he lay dying, Maxine left the room and returned with a camera. She walked around him, eyeing up the shot from different angles.

"Need to get the frame right," she explained, "Don't want the farewell photograph I'm taking for my cousin to look like it's been shot by an amateur."

Click. "Perfect."

Notes on
'Body in the Bracken'

Revelstoke Drive is a wide track that runs along the coast from Noss Mayo to Stoke Point with uninterrupted views of the sea as it gently follows the contours of the cliffs. It is part of a nine mile circular carriage ride built in the 1880s by the land-owner, Edward Baring, first Lord Revelstoke, to take his visitors on spectacular rides. He was, by all accounts, a very generous man and paid local out-of-work fishermen to construct the driveway. On completion, Baring asked them to make it three feet wider so as to keep them in employment.

Incidentally, under his leadership, Barings Bank collapsed and, unlike the bankers of today, he was held personally responsible and had to sell his land, home and possessions.

The old coastguard cottage, that is featured in this story, stands on the site of the Gunrow Signal Station, which was a communications system for the Admiralty fleet during the Napoleonic wars. Signal officers would alert neighbouring stations in the chain by means of semaphore flags hoisted on poles. The present, unoccupied, building dates back to the early 1900s and in the past has served as a coastguard lookout, a Second World War observation post and a National Trust shop and cafe.

Beware of the Rocks

It was a bright June day and my plan was to walk the South West Coast Path from Bolt Tail to Salcombe — a distance of around nine miles.

On climbing up from Soar Mill Cove I was fascinated by the strange rock formations that seem to grow out of the cliffs there; a rugged wilderness of rocky spires and pinnacles. Some look like animals, some like birds and others are weird humanoid shapes — headless bodies and bodiless heads. As I neared the top of the cliff, I stopped to check what my Guide Book had to say about these strange shapes.

'Metamorphic schist and hornblendes, formed during the Devonian period about 350 million years ago. The weather and primitive ocean currents, over eons of time, have shaped their strange forms.'

I made a note to check the vocabulary as soon as I got back to my lodgings.

On reaching the cliff top, I decided to stop for lunch. Warm sun, fabulous views — lunch stops don't get any better than this. As I was sitting there, feeling deep gratitude for the gift of such a wonderful day, I became aware of a most unusual noise. I pictured a ferocious dog trying to bite its way through a fence. The type of dog that might attack sheep . . . or even people. I got to my feet. If I was about to be assailed by a savage dog, I needed to be prepared. The noise seemed to be coming from the cliffs below me, and yet at the same time, it was all around me. It wasn't pleasant and

I hurriedly re-packed my rucksack and continued on my way.

The views were breath-taking and I stopped many times to take photographs; soon forgetting about the strange noise. There was no one else on the path — the stillness interrupted only by the wild ponies grazing the grassy plains above Steeple Cove.

Less than an hour later, as I walked on towards Bolt Head, I was surprised to see a man sitting cross-legged below the path, by the side of a large rock that looked very much like the head of a giant troll. He shouted to me and beckoned me down to where he was sitting amongst the gorse and the bracken. I wondered if he was in trouble. It seemed a very odd place to be resting up. Reluctantly, I left the path and carefully made my way down the overgrown hillside toward him.

He began to pull at his long, white beard as he asked me what I thought about the rocks. I told him what I had ad in my Guide Book, feeling rather pleased with myself for sounding so knowledgeable about a subject I had known absolutely nothing about less than an hour ago. He was very polite and did not interrupt me, but when I'd finished he began to shake his head and beckoned me closer.

"These rocks are not what you think," he said in a hushed voice, "they are alive. They have no eyes but they see. No ears but they hear. You must be careful."

I honestly did not know what to say. I was dumbfounded and not a little frightened by his odd manner. I looked up towards the cliff and then down along the shoreline, hoping to see another walker, someone who might provide an excuse for me to hurry away. There was no one.

"They are shape-shifters," he went on, "one minute a rock, the next appearing in their own, terrible form. They were driven to extinction when the Earth was young and suffered greatly, but they have memories as strong as the forces that forged them. And they long for life again and the return of their kingdom."

"Sounds fascinating," I said apologetically, "but I really must press on."

I turned to go.

"Please," he said, "spare me a few minutes to listen to my tale."

I turned back and saw a sadness in his eyes. Maybe he was just lonely and needed someone to talk to. I saw neither malice nor evil intent there and so, albeit reluctantly, I sat down beside him.

"It was Old Joe and Wailing Lizzy saw them first," he said, "The year was 1856 and they were walking back to their cottage after a night of beach combing. A Clipper had gone down the night before. Twenty men drowned and all the cargo lost. Until the tide turned that is and then it all washed up on the shore; bodies and all. Aye they got a fair bounty from that ship did Joe and Lizzy. But not even the two gold teeth they took from the captain's mouth was worth what they endured that night. Old Joe reported they were making their way home along the self-same path you were on when suddenly they heard such a roaring and spitting, enough to make them think a bull was on the loose. By all accounts, what they saw turned Joe's hair white. It wasn't a bull. It was a dragon climbing up out of the sea and spitting fire in the moonlight. Chances are, it was that one down there. Can you see it?"

I looked to where he pointed. Sure enough there was a formation that looked like some sort of weird sea monster dragging itself out of the sea — but anyone in their right mind could see it was just a rock.

He continued, "Now folk around at that time said Joe wasn't given to flights of fancy, nor exaggeration as far as they knew, so everything he said can be relied on. He said Lizzy, never one to keep quiet, started shouting and cursing enough to wake the dead. Joe told her to quiet herself, but it was too late. The dragon started towards them, pulling itself along with its stone claws, screeching and grinding on the rocks. It had Lizzy in an instant, clamped its huge jaws round her head and dragged her off into the sea. Joe never came up here again, not even in the daytime."

This was one crazy old man, I thought, but he had me rooted to the spot like the wedding guest in the Ancient Mariner. He went on with his mad tale.

"There was another two left this world in the mouth of the dragon that same year and another three in the 1960s. There's bound to have been others but unless there's witnesses, who's to say? All I'll say is that a tidy number of walkers have disappeared on this stretch of cliff, never to be seen again. But more worrying than the tales of the dragon is the great bird that is perched on top of the cliffs, looking out toward the sea. You'd have seen it as you climbed up from Soar Mill Cove. Did you see it?"

I confirmed that I had. In fact it had been the sight of that great rock that had caused me to check my Guide Book.

"That's an evil bit of work," he continued, "I've heard say that it's a more recent resurrection. The personification of a demon witch that once practised her evil deeds in Salcombe. That is until the Witchfinder General set a torch under her and burned her soul to Hell. That bird is enough to put the fear of God into all who walk this path and, as far as we know, it's due for its next meal."

"I'm sorry?" I laughed, hardly able to believe that he was telling me it might eat me!

"It last ate on June 13th last year," he continued without acknowledging my interruption.

'My God,' I thought, 'he's serious!'

"It was about thirty minutes past the hour of six and a good three hours afore the sun went down. There'd been backpackers up on Bolt Tail earlier that afternoon, heading east on the path hoping to catch the ferry to East Portlemouth. But they never made it. Their remains were found on the cliff the next day. They'd been pecked to pieces, nowt but a few bones and scrags of hair left."

The way he intoned that last sentence sent shivers down my spine and I was suddenly filled with a fear I could not explain.

"I really must go," I said, this time not giving him chance to persuade me to stay. I set off scrambling up the hillside towards the path.

"Mark my words," he shouted after me, "be on your guard or they'll have you."

On reaching the path, I set off running. I was alone with a crazy old man in the middle of nowhere and it was freaking me out. But the clamber up the steep hillside had left me exhausted and I soon had to slow my pace. I checked

my watch to estimate what time I would reach Salcombe —
I knew there were no other habitations along this stretch of
the path. It was almost six. How could that be? I had eaten
around two o'clock and I couldn't be much more than an
hour's walk away from the lunch-stop. Where had four hours
gone? I didn't want to stop and check my map so I put my
misgivings aside and hurried on whilst nursing a growing
fear, mingled with a dizzying sense of not being quite
present.

The sun was low in the sky as I climbed up Sharp
Tor. A large hole in the rock near the pinnacle seemed to be
watching me, like the vacant eye of some prehistoric
monster. It was a steep climb and I had to rest often.

As I approached the top, the rock began to move and
shudder under my feet. This was how I imagined an
earthquake would feel.

I grabbed the handrail for support and looked down
at the sea. The water seemed to be vibrating and an

unworldly, all-pervading silence hung over the land. The seagulls, that had been fighting and squalling down in Starehole Bay, were now silent. Even the ravens were gone from the cliffs. Then I heard someone screaming ahead of me and a man calling for help. I took a few more steps, but I could feel another tremor building and imagined the whole cliff falling apart. The handrail began to shake so I let go and clung to the rocks instead, trembling with fear. The man continued to shout, I couldn't ignore him. Crawling up the remaining steps on all fours, I bravely made my way to the rocky ledge at the top. The path was even narrower here and was littered with jagged rocks sticking up out of the ground. I eased my way round, clinging onto the rock for support.

When I turned the corner, I saw that part of the cliff had fallen away, taking the path with it and leaving behind a natural sculpture that looked like the face of a demon — horns and all. Inside its gaping mouth was a man, struggling to keep hold of jagged pinnacles of rock that looked like rows of razor-sharp teeth. What could I do? There was a huge, deep chasm between us that I could not cross.

I watched in horror as his grip loosened and he disappeared into the abyss. It was as if he'd been eaten by the Devil himself.

*   *   *

I haven't slept too well since then. The Doctor says I have post-traumatic stress. The nightmares are the worst — and the tablets don't seem to have any effect.

And the old man by the rock . . . I think about him a lot. I didn't notice at the time, with him being sat on the ground, but later I realised he was of very small stature. I'd even say dwarf-like. Was he a man? Or was he a spirit from the land come to warn me? I don't know what he was and I have no wish to find out. Strangely though, his shirt was the exact same colour as the bracken.

These past few days, I have felt compelled to follow his example and warn others of the danger of these rocks. So, if you are ever on that cliff and hear weird noises or happen upon this strange man, you would do well to leave the path immediately and head inland. Because . . . did I say? Three more walkers have disappeared in the last month. And there's something else — the Devil rock speaks to me in my dreams.

"I'm coming," it growls at me in the dead of night, "And I shall take back what is mine."

Notes on
'Beware of the Rocks'

The idea for this story was born from the actual rocks that are to be found on this stretch of coastline. They give the feel of a sentient landscape, especially when you are walking alone.

This part of the coast is also subject to slippage and sudden, catastrophic erosion, although this is far more apparent further along the coast as you approach Dorset. It was in Dorset that the idea for how this story was to end came to me. It was there, just like in my story, that I had a lucky escape.

The South West Coast Path goes through West Bay — the Dorset coastal town of *Broadchurch* fame, (*Broadchurch* is a popular, serialised UK TV drama) — and from there runs over East cliff. Just a few hours after I'd walked over East Cliff, torrential rain caused a large section of the cliff to fall onto the beach below, taking the South West Coast Path with it.

Tiger's Revenge

"We were sailing to Slapton Sands when it happened. I was in the 4th Infantry Division, and a long way from my home in Missouri. My company boarded one of the Tank Landing Ships at Brixham and joined the end of a three mile long convoy that had set sail from the Isle of Portland. It was Ultra-Top Secret — Exercise Tiger they called it — a rehearsal for an assault landing in Normandy. Though we didn't know that at the time — only found that out later from Lieutenant Barnaby, the commander of the other LST that went down. He had BIGOT-level clearance and spilled the beans to us as soon as he realised it didn't matter anymore.

We hadn't been at sea long when we heard talk that there were a couple of other boats in the area. The gaffers, in their wisdom, decided they were part of our escort and ignored them. Bloody navy! Bloody hotshots — flapping their lips non-stop and not a cent worth of common sense between 'em, no siree! They were only bloody German E-boats — nine of 'em! —alerted by the crazy amount of radio traffic there'd been all day. Well, we were done for — torpedoed as we circled round Lyme Bay. The Lieutenant commanding our ship hasn't been seen around here so I guess he must have survived. I hope he got his chops busted and got some time in the slammer. But I expect he found a Patsy to get him off the hook. That's what usually happens. If he were here now, I'd let him have it — geez — would I just!

As soon as we took a hit, Sergeant Brook was yelling at us to put on our life jackets. Well man, you try putting on a life jacket when you've got a forty-pound pack strapped to your back. We fastened them the only place they'd go — round our waist. Turns out they should have been tied round our back and chest. When I was blasted into the sea, the life jacket flipped me over like a turtle, forcing my head under the water. Same for hundreds of others. Oh boy! Catapulted out of this world and into the next.

They say death by drowning is peaceful — believe me, it ain't. It was gruesome. Geez — gasping for air when there was no air to be had, only the cold, stinging briny and the sea on fire all around us. Private Bully Brad, the knucklehead with the chrome-dome, said we were the lucky ones — at least we weren't killed by our own like he was. Somebody over here on this side called it friendly fire — Brad said there was nothing friendly about it. And all Eisenhower's fault. What sort of military outfit orders live ammo to be used for a practice run and can't even figure out the time difference between us and the Brits? Those that landed on the beach got mistaken for Germans because the clocks hadn't been synchronised.

And would you believe it, the small naval ships they'd sent to escort us were using a different radio frequency. That's why they weren't there to give us warning. When they eventually arrived, it was too late to help us. In fact, I heard some of 'em turned tail and scarpered like dogs with their tails on fire. It was a total screw-up and no mistake.

When I came to, I was lying at the bottom of the sea with my buddies, all in a heap and jumbled up like a load of rag dolls. It ain't fair, not when we died in the line of duty. And it's a hound dog shame because they're a great bunch of lads and no mistake. Damn brave men, the lot of 'em. Someone from across a great river came to talk to us the other day, told us we're not soldiers anymore — we're discarnate now, whatever that means. Said we need to move on.

I've been worrying about my Ellie May and the babe she was carrying when I died. Wondering how she's fared without me. Somebody over here — one of those with a weird light around them — told me she'd found herself a Gunner's Mate — perhaps she figured she'd be safer with him, but I heard he'd gone the same way. As for the baby, there's been no news. I've tried to look for Ellie May but it's hard when you're dead — things look different and you can never be sure where you are or what you're seeing.

Anyhow, we're getting hotshot bored down here and so the other night we all got together and decided on a plan of action. No one's going to like it — well not anyone that's living that's for sure — but it has to be done. Ghosts need rest, we can't spend all eternity in this torment, feeling like victims, feeling like we never mattered. Me and the lads, we thought we'd make the trip to Guz, Devonport they call it, on the next full moon — makes it more creepy that way. Scare the shit out of the bastards that were responsible for our demise. When the top brass heard what we were planning they said they'd join us.

The intention is to sail into the south yard. Second Officer Potter has said he can raise a spectre of one of the Tank Landing Ships and we'll all pile into that, all except the third squadron who will get inside the Sherman amphibious tank that's currently sitting in a car park at Torcross covered in tar. Andy Burnhill, the Chief Sapper (that's a navy engineer to you and me) is quite confident he can get it to Plymouth in good time for our arrival. He's on good terms with some real clever dicks over here who, he says, have made some holes and tunnels, like worms make in dirt. He reckons he can send it through one of those. Don't understand it myself but he seems to think it'll work."

*   *   *

"Well it all seemed to go to plan. We landed near a waterfront cafe — I couldn't make anything out but there are those among us who have the gift of sight and can see the living and what's going on. Most of us can only hear them. Well, not hear exactly. It's a sort of weird vibration that we pick up but it's easy to distinguish between people and animals — animals have a much lower pitch. When there's fear, the vibrations get really fast so that's how we knew we'd scared the bejesus out of the landlubbers.

There was just one problem — those blessed with the sight said it all looked different to how they remembered it. Said the ships weren't the sort of ships we sailed in, they were like nothing they'd ever seen before and they were pretty sure some of them were armed with what the Chief Sapper was calling atomic bombs. He reckons we must have been dead a long time but I can't believe that, it only seems like yesterday that I was trying to breathe water.

Some of us were directed by Lt Barnaby to board the submarines. I wasn't one of them, more's the pity. I was directed to an area referred to as the Barbican. I was part of a contingency following behind a seer. He told us to make as much noise as possible — stamp our feet and fling our arms about in anger. He said that would make more of a fright. I was amazed to discover I could move things, tables and such. Holy mackerel, I tell you, all the lads cheered when I managed to send something flying through the air. Cornish Pasty said it was a chair. Wish I'd seen it.

The amphibian arrived just after us — that was a sight and no mistake. Andy Burnhill and his crew looked to me to be floating through the air, but Cornish Pasty related every detail to us, how the tar-covered tank, with its ghostly crew, trundled over the cobbles, smashing into cars the like of which we'd never seen, and people screaming and running around in panic. I hope no one got hurt, wouldn't want that, there's been enough maiming and killing.

And then it happened. We all heard it. Some of us stopped our rampaging but others, being intoxicated with the excitement of it all, just carried on. It was them that were affected first. Can't really explain what happened. They sort of diminished in size — shouting and screaming they were, and there was a voice yelling at them to go towards a light that was shining over the Hoe. It was like they were being sucked away, protesting, not wanting to go. And then all the noise and clamour died down and Andy Burnhill, who had long since jumped down from the tank, said we should all go back to Slapton and lie low or we'd be going the same way. So that's what we did.

We've only about half our number now and we're all feeling a bit emaciated, thin as a balloon blown up too much, but we've had a meeting and decided that once we feel rested we'll have another go. I hear one of the real top brass from across the great river will be joining us. I've only seen him the once, and that from a distance. Short chap — scared the bejesus out of me and I'm dead so God knows what he'll do to the living. Cornish Pasty's seen him close up and said he looks strangely familiar, like someone he's seen before in the movies — somebody famous. One of the sappers said he seems like a regular screwball, yelling all the time in a foreign language that he thinks might be German. I hope it's not that bastard with the silly moustache."

Lt. Douglas Harlander, a US Navy survivor on LST 531,
> *'I estimate that at least two-thirds of those on board never made it off the ship and today their remains rest at the bottom of the English Channel.'*
> Source: 'The D-Day rehearsal that cost 800 lives' by Claire Jones BBC News Online http://www.bbc.co.uk/news/uk-england-devon-27185893

The Sherman amphibious tank that now stands in the car park at Torcross is a memorial to the men who lost their lives.
The operation to salvage the tank from the shallow waters of Start Bay was financed by Ken Small, a Torcross hotelier, and was completed in 1984.
Mr Small has told the story of Exercise Tiger, and his discoveries, in a book called *The Forgotten Dead*.

Notes on
'Tiger's Revenge'

In late 1943, Torcross was evacuated, along with many other villages in the South Hams area, to make way for 15,000 allied troops who needed the area to practice for the D-Day landings. Code-named Exercise Tiger, it took place in the early hours of 28 April 1944 and was a landing rehearsal using live naval and artillery ammunition to make the exercise as real as possible. The operation had BIGOT-level clearance, which was a codename for a security level beyond Top Secret. But the exercise went horribly wrong with loss of life greater than the actual invasion of Normandy just months later.

Nine German torpedo boats, alerted by heavy radio traffic, intercepted the three-mile-long convoy of vessels travelling from the Isle of Portland to Slapton Sands. Two Tank Landing Ships (LST) were sunk and almost a thousand servicemen died — many either because of lifejackets worn incorrectly or through hypothermia. A complete list of casualties is not available, but Army records, possibly not complete, state that 749 were killed and more than 300 either injured or suffered from severe exposure. It is believed that many more than is recorded perished that day. The 3206th Quartermaster Service Company sustained the heaviest losses and were more or less wiped out.

Poor communications also led to badly-timed shelling on the beach, resulting in many men being killed by friendly fire. The exercise was considered by the US to be such a disaster that they ordered a complete information blackout. Families of those who died were told that their loved ones were either killed or missing in action — they didn't discover the truth until the 1980s. One of the Tank Landing Ships, LST 507, is lying at the bottom of the sea and is a popular location for wreck diving.

The Naval base at Devonport is still nicknamed *Guzz/Guz* by sailors and marines.

The Empty Wall

Edmund sank to his knees in front of the empty wall —
hands clasped in front of him as if in prayer. A thunder
storm was lashing, raging at him, but he was oblivious. It
had cost him all his savings to come here, wiped him out, but
the need to feel close to her again had been too strong to
resist. And now . . . there was nothing; nothing but an empty
wall where she should have been.

She was all he had thought of for so long. It never
occurred to him that she wouldn't be here.

He stumbled to his feet, holding onto the wall for
support, afraid of falling. Bones that were once strong were
now as brittle as dry kindling and might snap if he slipped on
the wet path.

"You're very welcome to come inside the church," came a comforting voice from the shelter of a Yew tree. It was the Priest, braving the storm to see if the stranger needed help.

"Where's it gone?" Edmund asked, pointing at the empty space in the wall where her memorial stone should have been.

"I'm not sure, it disappeared quite some time ago. Please, we'll discuss this inside, out of the rain."

Edmund shook his head, "A church is no place for the likes of me."

"Everyone's welcome here," the Priest said, and added with a hint of mischief, "we're all sinners, even me."

"I'm no sinner," Edmund retorted, "yet I do have the mark of the Devil on me."

The Priest frowned. He seemed to be on the verge of asking Edmund to explain, but then plainly thought better of it.

"Well, if you change your mind, you know where I am," he said and hurried off back to the church. Edmund heard the key turn and the bolt slide home, a sure sign that he would no longer be welcome inside. A few seconds later a face appeared at the vestry window, gruesomely distorted by the rain.

The sudden aloofness of the Priest caused old memories to surface in Edmund's mind. He turned to look across the Dart estuary towards Kingswear. The opposite bank was nothing but a fading mirage, hiding in the sea fret that had blown in with the storm. Boats were bobbing up and down in the strengthening wind. They reminded him of the time they'd had together — happy times, the two of them in love and making plans for the future. He, a boat repairer, and she a beautiful young woman who healed the sick with herbs and potions — things that if given in too great a dose would kill instead of cure. But she was well schooled in the art and had saved many a soul from torment.

No one knew where she came from, not even him, but as the years passed the villagers began to notice that her youth was undiminished. If only things had stayed the same, if only she hadn't told him her secret.

Her confession, on a stormy day just like today, was still strong in his memory. She told him she was a witch of ancient lineage who fed on the dead to keep her youth. Said she had a gift for him — a gift he should have refused.

She took the life of the Radford boy and mixed together a potion of his fluids with the afterbirth from Mrs. Penny — the elixir of youth she called it, said it would slow his aging so they could have a long life together. It was shortly after that that the Preacher at St. Thomas's, too full of ale to keep his thoughts to himself, commented that she seemed to be getting younger with every death in the village. Word got round and people turned against her. There was talk of witchcraft.

The laws condoning the hanging of witches had been repealed in 1736 but the people of Kingswear were superstitious and took no notice. It was from the moorings that they threw her into the river at high tide, thumbs securely tied to opposite big toes. When she did not drown they tied her, half dead, to the boathouse gibbet.

As night fell and the villagers went to their rest, he untied her and ferried her over the river to St. Petrox where he held her in his arms and wept. With her dying breath she made him promise to return with a life not yet weaned so that, even after death, she might live again.

He buried her broken body inside the banking and returned the following day to shore up the grave with a tombstone from a stonemason in Dartmouth. But his promise to return had been over-shadowed by his terror at what he must bring back to her.

If ever there had been a time for honesty, it was then. He should have told her he had no stomach for murder and would not be able to do her bidding, no matter how much he loved her.

Instead, he fled the place, sailing over to the Americas to make his fortune. So very long ago. Forsaking her, denying her, abandoning her. She had been calling to him for over two hundred years, crying across the ocean, across the wild seas. Calling him home and he hadn't answered, hadn't wanted to listen, hadn't wanted to be reminded of what she had done — of what they had done.

"I'm sorry. Please forgive me," he cried, turning back to the empty wall. But the wall didn't answer and he set off toward Blackstone Point, intent on ending his torment.

Climbing up the rugged woodland track took more energy than he had and he stopped frequently, breathing heavily, trying to catch his breath. The mist was creeping through the trees like a hesitant shroud, twigs snapping, wind moaning. He could feel her close but could not see her. Every so often he cried out in anguish as the trees swayed around him.

"Where are you my love?"

At last he heard the answer in the sighing of the wind, "I have crumbled to dust for you have forsaken me."

"I have not forsaken you. I am here."

"Too late. Too late," the wind sang as it whistled through the trees.

"Come with me," he said, "for my time is at an end."

"Assured be, I shall be there," replied a voice that was colder than the fog.

*   *   *

On reaching Blackstone Point, he stood on the cliff edge, looking out across the wild grey sea as it sent plumes of white spray into the air around Western Blackstone. If there had been an easier way, he would have taken it. But there was not. 'Besides,' he thought, 'this is befitting a man who all those years ago looked across the ocean for his salvation.'

He stepped closer to the edge, the rain lashing at his face. The wind was fierce, blowing in from the ocean, he would have to leap strongly if he was not to have a slow death, injured on the cliff face.

Should he jump or dive? Jump — he could get more clearance that way. Where from? Indecision had him immobilised as he looked this way and that, searching for the best place. He wasn't a brave man and this would take every last morsel of courage.

At last he chose a place and paced out twenty steps from the edge — he would feel more empowered if he ran to his doom. Turning back to face the sea, he steeled himself for this last act.

He hit the water well away from the cliff, causing a sparkling plume to shower the air around him. He would have sunk but the wind had filled his lungs and he found himself bruised and tossed about like a piece of waveson. Above his thrashing body, came a white mist tinged with purple and filled with lightning flashes that crackled like spring swealings.

"I gave you the life of another so you could live in youth for an un-natural time," came her voice into the confusion of death, "the witch-haters destroyed me and you did nothing. You left me trapped in this abominable place, trapped inside the cold hard stone of death."

'I could not kill, not for myself and not even for the one I love.' Thus were his thoughts for the cold sea had silenced his voice.

"Then you shall never rest," she answered, "you shall die a thousand deaths and a thousand more until the end of time."

He felt the icy water enter his lungs, filling them up, suffocating him as the waves buffeted and churned him down into the black depths of Hell. She followed him, swirling around him in a violet haze, eyes white, black mouth agape.

"Bring me sacrifices," she said, "and with every sacrifice you shall be spared one death."

Thus he promised again to do her bidding, but this time there was no reneging and no salvation.

*   *   *

When at last the rain stopped, the Priest emerged from his place of refuge and hurried towards a crumpled heap on the stone pathway in front of the empty wall.

It was the old gentleman he had spoken to earlier. Cold as the grave with a look of terror on his face and something in his mouth that looked like seaweed. The Coroner confirmed this fact and said it was the sort of weed found a little further down the coast in Deadman's Cove. There was no explanation of how it got there.

There followed talk in the parish that the man had been un-naturally old and had returned to put a curse on the town, for many walkers followed Edmund to the grave on that stretch of coast. Accidents of course — a fall on a slippery path, a tumble down a long flight of steps in the woods, standing too close to the crumbling edge above Deadman's Cove or blown from the cliff up on Blackstone Point.

So if you are ever in that area and hear the sound of wailing in the tree tops, hurry on my friend, for dying once was more than enough for Edmund and, unlike the living, the dead do not dishonour the promises they have made.

View of St. Petrox Church from across the Dart estuary. The church, with its 12th century square tower, stands directly behind Dartmouth Castle.

Notes on
'The Empty Wall'

After a long day's walk of eleven miles, what a joy it was to come upon St. Petrox Church. A beautiful Grade I Listed Building nestling on the banks of the River Dart immediately behind Dartmouth Castle. Such an evocative place; I was intrigued to find out more about it.

The earliest reference was in 1192 when it was referred to as the 'Monastery of St Peter', though it is thought a religious structure may have stood here before then. The 12th century tower may have been built more as a watch tower than as a church, standing as it does right at the mouth of the estuary. The building itself has been added to over the centuries and contains 15th, 16th and 17th century additions. It is dedicated to a Welsh aristocrat named St Petrox — who is reputed to have given up worldly things and travelled to Ireland to study in piety.

On the day of my walk it had been raining hard but, as I came down from the cliff past Sugary Green, the sun came out and a leisurely stroll around the grounds of St. Petrox Church was just too tempting to resist.

I wandered over the wet paths, reading the inscriptions on the memorial stones set into the wall — shown in the photograph at the beginning of the story. As I moved along the path, I came upon an empty space where clearly there had once been a memorial stone and now there was none. Just at that moment, the sun disappeared behind the blackest of clouds and the rain started again.

I took refuge inside the church and the peaceful solitude I found there, invited this story to unfold in my mind.

Finding Napoleon

It was my misfortune to have Mr. Sinclair as a colleague. Being one of the land-owning and economic elite of Torquay, he was now a 'provincial patriot' of the war and had even organised a route-march to try and drum up enthusiasm in the men of Torbay to enlist in the National Reserve. He said the low recruitment figures were damaging Devon's patriotic reputation. In truth, he was a bigoted man whose most pleasurable pastime was belittling all who disagreed with him. Only this morning, he had been pontificating again.

"This war, David," he said, "is a necessary evil. The world must rid itself of the scourge of blood-lusting devils. And mark my words, the British people and the King's Commonwealth shall be victorious. We shall be glorified."

I asked him how anyone or anything could be glorified with a hundred thousand dead and a hundred thousand more waiting to die. He answered, with his usual lack of understanding, that it was the duty of every able-bodied man to fight and, if necessary, die for King and country. He had the misfortune of having been born with a deformity to his foot and, thus, was excluded from the term able-bodied. No doubt to his relief.

"Fiddlesticks!" I replied, "I'll fight if I must but I will not volunteer. If it was my intention to end my life, I would rather throw myself off the pier here in Torquay, not go willingly into France to have my head blown off in the squalor of the trenches."

Mr Sinclair's face turned beetroot red at that point.

"Traitor. That's traitors' talk," he spat. "You'd have been hanged for talking like that a hundred years ago!"

I continued with my attack, "You are luring the young men of Devon to their deaths under the misapprehension of winning honour and returning home a hero. Tell me," I demanded, "what glory is there in dying of trench fever in a muddy battlefield on the Western Front, or even worse, sent back home with limbs missing and your hands shaking so badly that you cannot even hold a cup?"

All the while I was speaking, Mr. Sinclair was blowing out his ample red jowls, preparing for his *attaque au fer*.

"Rumours! Nothing but rumours, and you should be ashamed of yourself for spreading them. The men of this town are morally obliged to uphold the proud reputation of Torquay. Volunteering is a test of manhood. Something you are clearly lacking."

"Open your eyes man," I was yelling at him now, unable to contain my anger. "Can you not see what's going on? Can you not read between the lines of the articles and the photographs that fill our newspapers every day?"

He was trying to interrupt me but I would not let him — not until I had spoken my piece. I continued, hardly pausing for breath.

"Why don't you go and speak with the brave men who lie in our hospitals, physically and mentally broken with the horror of Gallipoli? And they are the lucky ones. They tell of comrades blown to pieces or dying of fever in the hot wet mud of the trenches which, by the way, are overrun with swarms of black corpse flies. It is people like you that are killing our young men, not the Germans!"

That was all I had to say. Perhaps it had been too much.

"How dare you speak in this way?" He retorted. "I shall report you to the Town Council. See what they think of your treachery!"

The conversation was over. He, red and flustered, dashed off to write a report of my transgression. I was so angry, my heart was thumping in my chest, raising my blood pressure to such heights that I could feel it pounding inside my head. War, with its defeats and victories, its pain and devastation, was a dark cloud hanging over humanity, threatening to wrap itself around us like a shroud.

39980   PRINCESS GARDENS. TORQUAY

A stroll on a balmy Summer evening, surrounded by the smiling faces of strangers, was just what I needed after this tiresome day. It had been three long weeks since I last set foot in Princess Park and I breathed in deeply to enjoy the aroma of all manner of fragrant flowers. They warmed my heart and calmed my spirit. I was even in the mood for tilting my hat at passersby, and uttering pleasantries about our good fortune at being blessed with such a splendid evening. But then a group of soldiers appeared on the path before me. Was there no getting away from this wretched war? I escaped through a gap in the hedge before they reached me and walked down to the Promenade. The sea was glistening in the evening sunshine and I strolled up and down for a good half an hour, enjoying the laughter of boys daring to swim in the chilly water, squealing with every splash. There was a dog with them and they were trying to entice it into the water. It was having none of it; clearly having more sense than the boys.

I continued on to the Pavilion and was just about to take the path that leads past the green when I heard a man's voice. It was hushed as though frightened of being overheard and yet it was clear the man was quite distraught,

"Napoleon. Napoleon. Where are you? Napoleon. Is there no one who can help?"

The voice seemed to be coming from beyond the bushes.

"Hello?" I called, "Can I be of assistance?"

"Help me," the voice again, now rasping and hoarse. The urgency of it caused me to hurry back the way I had come in order to find a path that would take me to the other side of the hedge. It took minutes, only minutes, but when I got to where I thought the man would be, there was no one. All was silent. How very strange.

I continued with my stroll but did not see nor hear anything further that concerned Napoleon.

On reaching the Pavilion café I partook of some refreshment and took pleasure in sitting outside, watching the finely dressed ladies enjoying their evening stroll on the arm of their husband or betrothed.

"Excuse me, Sir," a voice that was both sweet and hypnotic, interrupted my reverie. The sun was low in the sky and was directly behind her but I could see she was a young lady of fine breeding. There was a look of helplessness and desperation on her face.

"How can I be of assistance, madam?" I enquired, politely lifting my hat.

"It's my little dog," she said tearfully. "He's run off and I cannot find him anywhere. I saw you arrive by the path from the promenade and I'm wondering if you saw him?"

She was a striking woman, about ten years my junior and expensively dressed in an elegant grey suit that flattered her tiny waist and small, neat hips. Her hat, decorated with the palest of orange roses, lay at a somewhat awry angle. I could see that she was greatly distressed by the disappearance of her dog and, understandably, was giving little thought to her appearance.

"I did see a dog down by the seashore," I said, "but he was with some boys and looking like he belonged to them. I can't even tell you what sort of a dog he was, I didn't pay much heed. But please, don't distress yourself, I will be most happy to assist you in your search. What is the little fellow's name?"

"Napoleon. He is called Napoleon."

"Ah well, that explains an earlier encounter. I heard a man calling for your dog. Your husband perhaps?"

The lady flushed, "Oh no, Sir. I'm not married, nor promised. I don't know who that gentleman could have been."

"Well, no matter. Come, let us begin our search. What breed of dog is Napoleon?"

She smiled gently, "He's a spaniel with a beautiful coat of the darkest brown. I love him dearly. I will be very upset if I cannot find him before dark."

"Then we must hurry. Here, take my arm."

Slipping her arm through mine, we set off in the direction of the promenade. It seemed a trifle indiscreet to ask questions of the lady and, thus, take advantage of her predicament, but there were so many questions hovering on my lips, eager to be given voice. Perhaps once her dog was found, she would welcome an invitation to dinner the next evening, or perhaps the theatre, whichever she preferred. The truth was that she had, without knowing it, stolen my heart.

As we walked, she confessed that the dog did not belong to her. It belonged to her brother.

"He answered the call to go to war," she said, "I begged him not to go but he wouldn't listen."

Her voice faltered and she stopped walking, "I received a telegram last week to say he had been killed on the front line. Now I have no one, he was my only family. It is more than I can bear. And Napoleon was so precious to him. My brother will not rest in his grave if Napoleon is lost."

Her eyes, of the softest blue, reddened round the rim and a large tear fell onto her exquisite porcelain cheek. Her grief tore at my heart. I wanted so much to comfort her and ease her distress.

"We will find him," I assured her, "I promise."

It was all I could do; etiquette forbade me from doing more. She smiled. Even though her eyes were full of tears, they were also full of love, though perhaps they only reflected what was in my own eyes.

We found Napoleon a short while later, down by the water's edge. A cute little thing, barking and running backwards and forwards along the shoreline, chasing the boys. It was clear that he was the dog I'd seen earlier.

"Napoleon," I shouted, "Here boy. Come on."

The dog bounded toward me, yapping, eager to be stroked. I handed the dangling lead to his mistress but she shook her head.

"You hold him for a while. Please."

He was wet and full of sand, I imagined she didn't want to spoil her fine clothes. We headed back towards the café.

"Now we have found your charge," I said, "I wonder whether you would do me the honour of accompanying me to the theatre tomorrow evening?"

She stopped and turned to face me.

"I'm sorry," she said. It was then that I saw something very strange in those soft blue eyes, something I did not understand at the time. I expected them to be full of relief at finding the dog, instead I saw only sorrow and confusion.

"I have to go now," she said, "I have delayed too long already. But I want you to promise me something?"

"Anything, my dear. What is it?"

"I want you to promise me that you will look after Napoleon, for he is everything to me and the only thing I have left. Will you do this for me?"

"But, why? . . . I can't . . . why do you ask this of me?"

"I have to go away. I can't say where."

"But this is madness. I don't even know your name. You can't just expect a complete stranger to —"

"Please, there is no time to argue. Please, I'm begging you. Please."

She was becoming terribly distressed and I had no choice but to give her my solemn promise that I would love and care for the dog as if it were my own. As soon as I had given her my oath, she turned to go and Napoleon pressed his body flat to the ground, pinning his ears back and whining softly. I reached down to stroke him and offer words of comfort. When I looked up again to watch her walk away, she was already gone, as if she had never been.

I was stunned, confused, shocked by the strange encounter. I wondered who she was and if I would ever see her again. Surely, she would come back for her dog. But how could she? She had never even asked my name. For my part, I knew I would never forget her. Those blue eyes would haunt me for the rest of my life.

Napoleon was looking at me like an orphaned child whose world has suddenly come apart. It caused me an overwhelming feeling of terrible melancholy, such as I had never experienced before. With a heavy heart, I set off back to my accommodation in the fading light, with Napoleon dutifully trotting at my heels. I doubted my Landlady would respond well to my having acquired a dog but I was sure, if I explained what had happened, she would at least be understanding and give me time to find alternative rooms.

When I reached the Promenade, I heard a dreadful commotion ahead of me and saw a gathering of people on the beach close to the pier. A policeman was in their midst, blowing his whistle and frantically pushing back the onlookers, including the boys I'd seen swimming earlier.

There was a body lying on the sand. My first thought was for the boys. How dreadful if one of them had been drowned. I quickened my pace thinking I might be of assistance. But then I saw it, bobbing up and down on the incoming tide — the hat adorned with the pretty orange roses.

I hurried onto the beach and pushed my way through the growing crowd of people. There she was, lying face down in the sand, hair undone and ragged, and her neat little jacket ruffled into a tight crumple.

"Keep back, Sir, there's a good chap." The policeman said, "There's nothing you can do. The lady's already dead."

"What happened? How did she die?"

"Drowned," the policeman said very matter-of-factly. "Suicide I reckon. Must have jumped off the pier. The water's deep there, it's a good spot. She's not the first and she won't be the last."

"But I was speaking with her only a few minutes ago."

The policeman shook his head, "You must be mistaking her for someone else, Sir. Judging by the state of the body, I'd say she's been in the water a good few hours."

"But I tell you, I was just speaking with her."

"And I'm telling you, you're mistaken. Now move along please Sir, we've a job to do here. And will you please quieten that dog, can't hear meself think!

*   *   *

Things were never the same after that. I had to move from my rented rooms, where I'd had the most marvellous sea view, into far less salubrious lodgings — a large house that accommodated a variety of tenants with a whole variety of pets. But I had given my word and was not about to break it. She was always in my thoughts and the love she had felt for that little dog reminded me of the lack of love in my own life. I began to think constantly of what I craved but would never have. Each day I struggled to reconcile the glorious potential of life with its stark, empty reality.

The following February, the Military Service Act came into force and brought in conscription. I applied for deferment on the grounds that I was engaged on important war work but Mr. Sinclair was now an agent of the state — a self-appointed arbiter of social morality — and he was sitting on the Tribunal that day. Not being in any way impartial, he pronounced that individual sacrifice was every man's patriotic duty if we were to ensure the national survival, and I was summarily dispatched to Flanders.

As Napoleon's fate was intimately bound to my own, a new home with the National Canine Defence League was looming on his horizon. Mr. Sinclair heard of this and offered to take charge of the little dog. He lived in a well-appointed house up on Vane Hill and insisted, most strongly, that he could do with the exercise and that walking a dog every day would be most beneficial. So the day before my departure, I took the little orphan to his new life of luxury. He didn't seem very pleased. As I waved him good-bye, he stood motionless on the well-manicured lawn, looking doleful, head on one side and whining pitifully.

*   *   *

The battlefields were Hell. I endured horrors that were far worse than I could ever have imagined. After two years, I returned to Torquay with one less leg than I had before, and the Red Cross Hospital, housed in the Town Hall, became my temporary residence. Sleeping was difficult. Despite medication, I awoke many a night screaming and in great distress. My comforter was Nurse Munroe and it was she who told me what had happened to my former colleague.

"Your Mr. Sinclair," she said to me one night when all the other patients were asleep, "was walking his dog at the far end of the pier." Her tone was hushed and secretive, reminding me of the stranger who had stolen my heart when I was a whole man with a bright future. "A gust of wind caught a lady's hat. Beautiful hat it was, with pretty orange roses all around the brim. By all accounts the dog went wild, running round and round in circles, chasing the hat and yelping. Mrs. Busby, who works at the ice cream stand, said the dog's leash wrapped itself around Mr. Sinclair's legs. With him having a clubfoot, he was a tad unsteady on his feet anyway, and when the dog jumped off the pier after the hat, he took Mr. Sinclair with him." Sally crossed herself at this point.

"He's dead then?" I asked.

She nodded, "Drowned."

"And the dog? What happened to Napoleon?"

"Oh you've no need to fret on that score. Once in the water, little Napoleon managed to slip his leash and scramble on top of the hat that was bobbing about on the incoming tide. He lives with me now. I'll bring him in to see you tomorrow if you like."

Notes on
'Finding Napoleon'

'Provincial Patriots' were the land owning, economic elite of Devon who, at the start of the First World War, were involved in trying to recruit men into the National Reserve. But recruitment was low. Devonshire men were farmers and fishermen and were, understandably, only concerned with their own survival.

Around the time of the Zeppelin raid over London, in October 1915, Lord Derby introduced the Derby Scheme. It was 'one last effort to uphold the voluntary principle'. Route marches were organised, displaying propaganda and appealing to men's ego and manhood.

It didn't have the desired effect and so Asquith's coalition government, on the 10th Feb 1916, passed the Military Service Act. This brought in the enforced conscription of unmarried men and widowers without children or dependents in the age group 18 - 41. The Act didn't apply to those in patriotic professions such as those engaged on important war work.

This was quickly followed, in May1916, by a second Military Service Act which extended conscription to ALL men aged 18 - 41 regardless of profession or circumstance. Deferment could be applied for if there were adequate grounds but applicants had to appear before a Tribunal, which was made up of the Provincial Patriots — who were renowned for putting service to country before individual or family needs.

A Christmas Demon

Malcolm was standing in his usual place at the bar of the King's Arms in Regent Gardens, hand caressing a pint of lime and soda. He looked relaxed and well turned out in the jacket he kept for best.

Shuffling a little to his left, he checked that his reflection was dead centre in a circle of twinkling Christmas lights that bordered the mirror behind the bar. His fedora was pulled slightly down over his forehead, hiding his receding hairline. Someone once told him that it took twenty years off him so he never went anywhere without it. The 'Dolce and Gabbana' shades looked ridiculously out of place, but he wore them because they added to the mysterious persona he was trying to cultivate. Turning his head, this way and that, he studied his reflection and thought how much he looked like Van Morrison. He scowled moodily to acknowledge his imagined audience.

He was on the look-out for a lover; someone to care for him, it's what his mother would have wanted. There had been four young women at the bar earlier and he'd gone over to talk to them. After giggling, in that horribly derisive manner that some girls have, they had turned their backs on him and told him to go away. His faded blue denims, tight as a drum, had been straining across the bulge that was growing there, and had caused the zipped fly to slide southward, exposing his Calvin Klein's, which were always black because he thought black was sexy. This exposure was a regular occurrence until the Landlord had pulled him up about it last month — said it was upsetting the pensioners who came in for their U3A meetings. Since then, he had got into the habit of feeling his crotch to make sure his fly was decent. But the girls were all breasts and thighs and he had forgotten to check. Sharon, the barmaid, accused him of being a 'perv'. The Landlord said he just needed a good woman to keep an eye on him.

And the Landlord was right. But finding a good woman was a lot harder than the Landlord seemed to think. There weren't many of them about. The good ones were already taken. The thought of his last failed encounter caused his hand to move involuntarily to a heavy metal cross that was safely tucked inside a concealed pocket inside the lining of his jacket. Until his mother's untimely demise, it had hung above her bed, and over her mother's bed before her. Both women had been good Christians and raised him in the faith.

"Spare the rod and spoil the child," his Grandmother used to say whilst she was beating him with a leather belt for the smallest misdemeanour. Regardless of that, he respected them for the sacrifices they had made and the cross was a constant reminder of their stalwart adherence to Christian values. Besides, he was plagued with disturbing visions since his mother's death and the cross made him feel safe; it was his protection. It was also his refuge and reassurance whenever his faith was challenged, as had happened last summer.

He'd been sunning himself on the promenade when an elderly couple, riding tandem on a mobility scooter, had stopped at the bottom of a small incline on the walkway. Malcolm watched them, not without some amusement, as the woman dismounted and removed a walking stick that was tucked between the seats. With great difficulty, she began staggering up the slope towards him. The man, meanwhile, leisurely tugged up the slope on the scooter and stopped at the spot where Malcolm was sitting.

"Not enough juice left in the old girl to get up this incline with the wife on," he explained. "You on holiday?"

On learning that Malcolm lived in the town, the man pulled a 'War Cry' from his pannier and asked Malcolm if he would be interested in reading it. Malcolm thanked him and said that he would. His mother had always given generously to the Salvation Army and been an avid reader of their magazines. Besides, the man had a kind face and Malcolm was relieved to have found a fellow Christian on whom to offload his burdens. He told the man about his disturbing visions and asked him what he thought he should do about them.

"Go and see your Doctor," the man advised, with an air of authority that Malcolm didn't like at all.

"But visions are a gift from God," he replied defensively, "surely it's our Christian duty to honour them and act on them according to God's word."

"Tell me son," the man said, "what exactly do you see when you have these visions?"

"I see the darkness in people's souls," Malcolm replied, "and I can see the demons that cling to them."

By this time the man's wife had joined them and both of them began shaking their heads and tut-tutting in such a way as to make Malcolm quite agitated. His mother's cross, which that day was inside his shoulder bag, began to feel very heavy. It always did when it sensed it might be needed. He nestled it closer to him.

"You need to go and see a Doctor, luv," the woman said, patting his hand in a way that was irritatingly patronising, "There are pills for that."

He put forward his evidence but they dismissed his claims without discussion and instead invited him to their regular Sunday meetings up on Brunswick Street. He firmly declined. He wasn't interested in organised religion and had no desire to go along and be preached at. Yet the couple had a warm light around them, with no hint of darkness, and there was something about the woman that reminded him of his mother, especially when she asked how much he drank. That was a question his mother used to ask all the time.

"Alcohol is the Devil's water," the woman scolded. "Stay clear of it."

The fire in her eyes when she spoke those words made him suspect that she had channelled his mother's spirit and so, the following day, he joined Alcoholics Anonymous. That was the reason he was drinking lime and soda on Christmas Eve. Sometimes though he would order a tot of vodka and slip it into a soft drink. No harm in that; it was only now and again.

The Landlord knew about his visits to A.A. and had sharp eyes, but he also had a mind to his profits and so his tongue was quiet. What the Landlord didn't know, however, was that Malcolm had an emergency stash at home, hidden in his cellar. He raided it whenever the last haunting memory of his mother roared into his head like a tsunami, trying to wash him away. Unlike the demons, that vision was colourful, like watching a film — the open head wound with white, bubbly stuff inside, and the pink carpet slowly turning red.

The vodka and his mother's ghost were just two of the demons he carried on his shoulders.

As the clock slowly turned towards ten o'clock, the pub began to fill and the growing crowd was jostling for a position at the bar. Reluctantly he moved away to let the alpha males join the feast.

His eyes were drawn to a woman standing in the doorway talking to two young men, not much more than boys. One of them handed her a drink and then they both kissed her on the cheek and wandered off to join others of their own age. He watched as she gently wove her way through the milling crowd and perched herself on a stool against the back wall, in a most dignified way. He admired that in a woman. Dignity. He pushed his way back to the bar and ordered two Sambuca shots. Sharon, the barmaid, frowned at him but said nothing. With a drink in each hand he sauntered over to where the woman was sitting and offered her one of the drinks.

"For you," he said, "for Christmas."

She smiled but then her eyes dropped to his fly and she raised her eyebrows. He feigned embarrassment.

"Sorry," he said, "new jeans. No free hands. Bit of a nuisance. I'm Malcolm."

"I'm Lucy."

"Please . . . take it," his arm was still outstretched, offering the Sambuca, "I don't mean any harm. I noticed you sitting here all alone. Just trying to be friendly."

She smiled again, it was a smile he could fall for.

"Thank you," she said, taking the drink.

"I haven't seen you in here before," he said, quickly zipping up his fly.

"My sons' idea. I don't really go out much."

"I hope you don't mind me saying, but there is sorrow in your aura. I have the sight for it you see."

"I beg your pardon?"

She sounded defensive — he would have to be careful.

"I'm an Evangelist, a disciple. Born again in the light of Christ. I see things other people don't see."

"I have an open mind," she said, "but not so open that my brains have fallen out!"

He thought her response quite clever but rather rude and it caused his first impression of a well-bred, dignified woman to be revised.

He touched the demon that he could see sitting on her left shoulder, "It's sitting here, it's only small, but it's holding on tight."

"You're weird," she said, drawing away, but he held her gaze. That was another of his talents.

"It came from a cottage with a red door," he said.

He saw her eyes fill with tears and it sent a victorious tingle down his spine.

"I'm sorry," he said, "I don't mean to pry. I'm not weird, I'm a healer. You've been treated badly with false promises of love. I see it; a little rag doll that's been tossed about too much."

His sympathetic insights always intrigued vulnerable women, making them want more.

"Let me get you another drink," he said. "My apology for seeing what you didn't want me to see."

When he returned with more shots of Sambuca, her eyes were dried and she was smiling again.

Taking the drink, she asked him why he was wearing sun glasses. Now it was his turn to get sympathy. He told her his eyes were sore and raised a finger in the air, indicating that she should listen to the music blasting out from the juke box. It was the band 'Mud' lamenting a cold and lonely Christmas. She was looking at him now the way people look at stray dogs.

"I know what it's like to spend Christmas alone," she said, "I worked for the Samaritans for a while."

"I thought you weren't supposed to tell people that?" he said. The colours in her aura changed slightly. He had embarrassed her. He knew about the rule of confidentiality because he too had worked for the Samaritans, though they had asked him to leave when he had been overheard telling a caller to be sure to renounce the devil before taking his own life.

"I'm sorry," he said, taking her hand, "I didn't mean that as a criticism."

His words made the red fade, and a thin green ribbon of light swirled over the top of her head, making the demon on her shoulder shrink a little. He knew what that meant.

"You're lucky," he went on, "you've got a lovely day planned for tomorrow. Friends coming round, lots of laughter and Christmas cheer. I can see it."

That did the trick. The red in her aura disappeared completely, replaced by a soft green hue.

"What about you?" she asked. "What have you got planned?"

He shrugged his shoulders and made sure his expression was as doleful as a blood hound.

"Where do you live?" she asked.

"Just around the corner, not far."

"Tell you what," she said, "I hate to think of anyone alone on Christmas Day. Why don't you come to mine for dinner tomorrow?"

He made noises of protestation whilst making clear it would save him from his wretchedness.

"Won't your sons mind?" he said, delving for more information.

She waved her hand in their direction, "They don't live with me, flown the nest a while ago, and it's their father's turn this year."

She patted his hand in reassurance. It caused a strain inside his jeans that made him feel sweet and full and ripe.

"You won't be on your own with me," she laughed, unaware that her words would disappoint not reassure. "There'll be six of us, all singles, so you'll be quite safe."

Malcolm hid his disappointment well and offered to get more drinks. They were soon laughing together like old friends. It had been such a long time since he had met anyone interesting enough to share an evening with.

"Come away with me for the New Year," he said, hoping she too had romance on her mind, "to the Highlands of Scotland, where eagles fly. We can share a sunset and I'll hold your soul in my arms until dawn."

That usually wove its magic immediately, so he was surprised when her answer was rather negative.

"It's a bit too soon to be talking like that," she said.

"We'll see," he said, slipping his arm around her waist and giving her a squeeze. He felt her muscles tighten and she edged away from him. He wasn't too concerned, he was sure she would come round.

When time was called, her sons jumped into taxis — the clubs in Torquay were open all night. He offered to walk her home. At first, she said no, but he was very insistent, said it wasn't safe for a woman walking alone at this time of night. At last she accepted.

As they crossed Regent Street he took her hand but she shook it free. Then he tried to kiss her but she pushed him away and didn't walk so close to him after that. He asked her why she was being so distant and she mumbled something about not being religious and wasn't sure she wanted to be Bible-bashed. That was one cliché that he found very insulting. The metal cross, tucked inside his jacket, suddenly became much heavier.

At last they came to the open area of The Den. It was when she turned to him and asked him not to get the wrong idea about her that the anger started gnawing at his insides. Her dismissive manner reminded him of his last girlfriend who had given him the brush-off just because he had tried to move their relationship forward into something a bit more intimate.

"You don't need to walk any further with me," she said, "I'm nearly home."

"I want to."

"Well I don't want you to."

The demon on her shoulder was laughing at him — it had grown back to its original size, knowing it had won the game.

"And I hate to do this," she added, without any trace of remorse, "but I'm also going to have to withdraw my invitation for tomorrow. I've just remembered . . . my sons are coming for dinner."

The demon on her shoulder began to jump up and down with joy; fists punching the air in victory. It was making her lie, making her deceive him. Malcolm yanked the metal cross from his jacket. One strike and Lucy collapsed into a bed of sugary-pink, winter Cyclamen that were nodding their heads at the side of the path. Another strike and the foliage turned the wonderful deep red of Poinsettia bracts.

He stood over her, looking down at her crumpled form with tears in his eyes. Another opportunity for love had been snatched from him. He could have exorcised the demon she had been carrying and they could have had such a good life together. But no, she had chosen the demon over him. Still, she was now healed — the demon had jumped onto his shoulders when life had left her.

He snuggled the cross back inside his jacket. The Catholic Church of St. Michael the Archangel was holding a midnight mass. If he hurried he might catch the Priest before he went home — he could offload the demon there.

He set off running along the promenade, with the sound of the sea in his ears and his mother's last scalding accusations inside his head.

'*You're crazy, son. You need help.*'

His mother, God bless her, had never understood that sometimes God's work is unpleasant for everyone and we can't always be nice people.

Notes on

'*A Christmas Demon*'

Teignmouth, on the north bank of the River Teign at the mouth of the estuary, is a popular holiday resort. I stayed here at the house of my friend's sister whilst walking the South Hams part of the path, so I had plenty of time to soak up the atmosphere of the place.

I was very tempted to write a story around Smugglers' Tunnel in Shaldon - an evocative place that conjures up all sorts of dark, dastardly goings on.

However, on walking through the town, I passed the Church of St. Michael the Archangel and thought immediately of a story I had already written about a man who became a 'Born again Christian' after claiming to have seen the Archangel Michael. He subsequently began to have visions of demons and felt it his mission to eradicate them from the world.

On seeing the Church, the Writing Guru that lives inside my head, insisted that I include that tale, suitably adapted for Teignmouth.

Return of the Eagle

It was 1976 — the summer that has been the benchmark for all hot summers since. It was a scorcher. The Labour government appointed Denis Howell as the 'Minister for Drought' and passed legislation to make it illegal to waste water. Hose pipes were banned — some areas were so dry they had communal standpipes. I remember Mr Howell inviting the press into his home and telling reporters that he and his wife were sharing baths to save water — that caused a few raised eyebrows I can tell you. It was rumoured that he had also done a rain dance on the orders of the Prime Minister. If he did, it worked. Only days later, thunder storms and heavy rain caused widespread flooding and he was renamed 'Minister for Floods'. I'm not sure we'd heard of global warming then — I think perhaps we had but governments weren't taking any notice.

Prior to the deluge, the weather was perfect for camping and so that's what we did — my husband and I — in a field somewhere near Sidmouth. One day, having tired of the beach, we went shopping in the town and wandered into a back-street antique shop with a brass bell on the door and a dusty smell of mothballs in the air. There was a wooden eagle hanging on the wall inside — positioned as if it was about to fly out of the grimy Georgian-style window. As soon as I saw it, I loved it and my heart yearned to set it free. I asked the price but the owner of the shop said it wasn't for sale. I pleaded, smiled, cajoled, but to no avail. Reluctantly, we left the shop empty-handed and went down to the beach to spend yet another afternoon sun-bathing below the crumbling cliffs.

But the eagle wouldn't leave my thoughts. That night, it flew into my dreams as I lay, restless, in my sleeping bag — soaring over mountains while soldiers fought and died in the valleys.

We went back to the shop every day to ask the owner if he had changed his mind but the answer was always the same, "No, it's part of the shop furnishings."

Then came the day we were leaving to go back home. I just could not leave without the eagle. It took a while to persuade my husband to drive round to the shop one more time. This time I went in alone and this time the owner said 'yes'. As he hooked it down from the wall he told me it had arrived in a consignment from Germany. I asked if it may have been from a church — perhaps part of a lectern. He said he didn't know but thought it may have been attached to a wardrobe. That was a bit disappointing but didn't detract from its aesthetic beauty.

When we got it home I positioned it as it had been in the shop — as though it was about to take flight through the window. The cat reacted very badly to that. He was Siamese and a big brute of a creature who was the embodiment of love and gentleness with me but who would regularly attack visitors he didn't like.

I remember when we first moved into the house, there had been an incident with the local vicar who had called to welcome us into the village. Comfortably ensconced on the settee, with his Bible in one hand and a glass of sherry in the other, he had no free hands with which to defend himself when Maximillian Proudpaws leapt onto his chest and placed a warning paw on each shoulder. After giving him a very long, and very intimidating, cat stare, Maximillian launched himself at the Vicar's nose, biting and drawing blood. The vicar screamed and ran away. We never saw him again but learned later that he had been transferred to another parish for interfering with the altar boys.

As for the eagle — as soon as Maxmillian saw it he sat and howled at it all night. At the time, we thought nothing of it and simply took it down, smeared it in cat mint and re-introduced it to our feline companion slowly. Still oblivious to its covert credentials, it became part of the furniture — its presence only seen and commented on by visitors.

In June 2017, I found myself in Sidmouth again. Twenty-eight years had passed since the fall of the empire that had been my marriage and I was walking the challenging South West Coast Path, alone. This particular day I had walked from Exmouth and, finding myself with an hour's wait for the 9A bus that would take me back to my accommodation in Lyme Regis, I had a coffee and spent some time wandering round, looking to see if there was anything I remembered from all those years ago. There wasn't, but I did stumble on a magnificent statue of an eagle, perched just a stone's throw away from St. Giles and St. Nicholas church.

It brought to mind the eagle that I had bought in Sidmouth all those years ago — a forgotten treasure, packed away in my attic after my latest house move and covered in mould the last time I saw it.

I took a photograph of the impressive statue before moving in closer to read the inscription on the plinth. Thus engaged, I didn't immediately notice the elderly gentleman who had come to stand beside me.

"Tragic, tragic," he muttered, shaking his head, "some of them were my friends."

"I'm sorry to hear that," I said, turning my head to look at him. His face was etched with the scars of life's troubles; weathered like a rough sea on a rainy day.

"War is tragic for everyone," I added, whilst thinking it was somehow paradoxical to have such a grand statue lamenting the dead and at the same time appearing to glorify war.

"I was the only one to come back," he said, "I opened an antique shop in the town. Always had a passion for eagles. So did you, if I remember rightly."

"I beg your pardon?" I heard exactly what he had said but was astounded by this insight.

"You bought an eagle from me . . . 1976 I think."

"How do you know that?" I didn't try to hide my astonishment.

"I have a good memory for dates and faces. I never forget a face."

I laughed nervously, "I haven't changed then?" My question sounded flippant but I was shocked and couldn't think of anything else to say. His face remained impassive.

"We all change," he said, "sometimes for the better, sometimes for the worse. It was one of a pair you know, that eagle of yours."

"You never said."

"The other one is still in the Black Forest where they were both created — carved in the 19th century from the trunk of an oak tree in Oppenau."

"You told me it was off a wardrobe."

"I lied. I'm sorry."

"So what is — how do you say — its provenance?"

"The pair were acquired by a wealthy merchant of dubious character in the 1950s. He died in 1975 and his chattels were distributed according to his wishes — the better pieces going to the monastery in Oppenau. The rest was bundled up into consignments and shipped off to the highest bidder with the proceeds going to various charities. The Eagle of Contrition was inadvertently placed into a consignment I had purchased. You'll remember I didn't want to sell it to you, but you were very insistent."

"Contrition? Like a penance or punishment?"

"In a way, yes. But more a punishment inflicted on oneself. The eagle isn't bad in itself. It doesn't make bad things happen. You do that yourself. Let's just say it makes you aware and remorseful."

I was puzzled. What was he saying? That the eagle had been affecting my thoughts for the past forty years?

"So why didn't you tell me this at the time?" I asked.

"I always intended taking it back to Germany," he went on, ignoring my question, "Reunite it with the Eagle of Abundance, its mirror image. That's what I felt it wanted. Yet . . . where do such thoughts come from? Sometimes it is prudent not to listen."

"I don't understand," I said, "Are you saying that the eagle spoke to you?"

"Eagles have no words to speak," he said with a grave expression. "But the Eagle of Abundance was once in Hitler's possession. So you make up your own mind about that."

He seemed to be talking in riddles.

"So you think that the other eagle can be used for personal gain?" I asked incredulously, "And that if Hitler had also possessed the Eagle of Contrition, he would have been filled with remorse and wouldn't have done what he did?"

The old man sneered, "Thoughts charge in and fill up the space between our ears like errant children in a playground. I can't comment on your thoughts, my dear, for they are your thoughts, not mine."

"So tell me your thoughts . . . please."

He shook his head and walked away, muttering something that sounded like a quote from the Bible. I watched him go, thinking him rather rude and wondering what I was doing hanging round talking to a crazy old man when I should be making my way to the bus stop at The Triangle. If I wasn't careful I'd miss the 17.34 and have to wait another hour for my ride.

Twelve months later

The hire car was waiting for me outside arrivals at Germany's Stuttgart airport — a brand new Opel Astra, which was a nice surprise. For what I was paying, I had expected an old beat-up Volkswagen or more worryingly, a Trabant — though I was aware that these would more likely be seen in the area that was East Berlin before the wall came down.

I set off heading south on the A81 and soon found myself totally captivated by the beauty of the Black Forest area. Swathes of dense, evergreen forests carpeted the softly rounded mountains; the embodiment of the gentleness and abundance of Mother Earth. Peppered here and there, were picturesque villages that spoke of community and kindness, offering their hospitality to any strangers that passed through. I was in no hurry to confront the purpose of my visit and so I stopped often to enjoy my adventure. In some ways, this was a business trip; an investment in my family's future, but there was no reason not to enjoy it.

It was early afternoon when I reached my destination; a monastery snuggled in a sizeable clearing deep within a forest, about three miles outside Oppenau.

As my car crunched to a halt on the gravelled track, a hooded figure raised its head from a vegetable plot and loosely waved an arm in greeting. I waved back but the figure was already bent again over his green charges. The monastery itself was surrounded by a high wall with heavy wooden gates that were open, giving access to an inner courtyard. I got out of the car and looked across to the vegetable garden again, hoping for reassurance that this is where I should go. But the monk now had his back to me and was lugging a heavy sack along the path toward an outbuilding that was leaning at a jaunty angle, as though it might collapse at any moment.

I ventured through the gates, my heart beating too fast and my breathing shallow. Since meeting the elderly gentleman in Sidmouth, it had become increasingly difficult to resist the temptation to re-unite the two eagles. It had made no sense at the time but the idea had grown in my head and it wouldn't leave me alone. Coincidences piled upon coincidences. Eagles were everywhere; they were even stalking me in my dreams. It was Boris the Golden Eagle at the Falconry Centre in Thirsk that finally decided me. The moment I saw him, he turned his head in my direction and never took his eyes off me. His Trainer commented that he appeared to have taken a fancy to me and I was promptly gloved and offered as a perch.

In the end, although this trip seemed a crazy extravagance, I figured I deserved a little abundance. There had been precious little of that in my life so far and the thought of acquiring the Eagle of Abundance became irresistible. It had got to the point where I was unable to think of anything else except travelling to the Black Forest to re-unite my eagle with its counterpart.

I had rehearsed so many times what I planned to say to Father Wilhelm, but every time my imaginings ended in confrontation. I wanted to buy his eagle but he wasn't selling. We had already corresponded by post as there was no internet connection in these parts, and he had made his position clear — the eagle was not for sale and not even for public view. Though I asked him why in several letters, he would never explain. It was frustrating to be met with such an obstinate refusal to even discuss it, and that was why I was here. I was hoping that a face to face meeting would clear the air between us, build some trust and, perhaps, get him to change his mind. After all, that strategy had worked in Sidmouth in 1976.

Passing through the gate, I entered a courtyard where sobriety hung in the silence. But then I noticed numerous empty oak barrels stacked against a wall, telling a somewhat different story. I wondered absently how much of the beer, which I knew they brewed, was consumed by the monks themselves. A crumpled figure, appearing from what seemed to be a small chapel, interrupted my thoughts.

"Welcome. Please follow," he said without introduction or ceremony.

I entered the chapel alone, the monk having stood aside and motioned for me to pass. A figure was standing at the far end, bent over a desk, preoccupied with whatever task he was engaged on. I assumed it was Father Wilhelm. There was not the barest hint of acknowledgement from him as I remained standing just inside the door, my eyes slowly growing accustomed to the gloom. He was writing in a heavy, leather bound book, swapping the pen from right hand to left and back again with alarming regularity. I thought it very odd. I coughed, hoping to attract his attention. He raised his free hand in a gesture demanding silence and carried on with his writing. I waited, respectful of the sanctity of the chapel. At last he placed the pen down on the open book and came towards me with slow, measured steps, hands clasped behind his back.

"Your journey is wasted," he said. His English was abrupt but excellent and perfectly understandable, which was fortunate as my linguistic skills were somewhat lacking. "I already have told you, the eagle is not for sale." His tone was authoritative and uncompromising.

"No, no," I lied, "I don't want to buy it. Just see it — perhaps photograph it?"

"No," he replied, "It is not on display."

I knew that it was. I had already done my research and Wikipedia had said that a carved 19th century eagle was part of the lectern which stood at the side of the altar in this very chapel. I glanced over at it, my eyes, by now, fully accustomed to the low light. It was hung beneath the reading shelf almost hidden from view by a velvet cloth of the deepest red. 'The colour of blood,' I thought. A large, ornate cross was embroidered in gold in the centre with the symbols alpha and omega at either side.

"What are you hiding?" I asked.

"We hide nothing."

I pointed over at the lectern, "It's there," I said emphatically, "Ever heard of the Internet? Wikipedia?"

"Please go. You are not welcome."

The edge in his voice betrayed his anger.

"I'm sorry, I don't mean to be rude," I said more gently, "Tell me have you heard of the Eagle of Contrition?"

He said he had not, but I suspected he was lying because, even through the gloom of the church, with its dim lighting and heavy atmosphere, I could see his eyes widen into an unblinking stare.

"I can show it to you if you like," I said, "It's in the car."

My words caused him great agitation, "No, I do not like. Go please."

"What are you afraid of?" I asked. "Do you not think the world deserves to share in your abundance?"

"There is no abundance here," he snapped, "We work hard. We have little. *Habgier wird der untergang der menschheit sein.*"

My very limited German immediately recognised *unter* — 'under' or 'down below'. The down below? The underground? The downfall?

By now, he had taken hold of my arm and was trying to escort me outside. His grip was strong and I knew there would be bruising to remind me of this encounter later. But he wasn't going to get rid of me that easily. I stood my ground, whilst trying to translate the rest of what he had said. Suddenly, the words the old man had muttered under his breath as we had parted company in front of the Sidmouth eagle, came back to me.

"He that hath ears to hear, let him hear."

I recognised it at the time as a quote from the Bible but hadn't given it another thought. Not so now. The smattering of German I had learned at school illuminated the words of Father Wilhelm and explained the reason for his odd behaviour. *Menschheit*, 'mankind'. And didn't *habgier* mean greed?

'Greed will be the downfall of mankind?' Is that what he had said?

It wasn't so much that I hadn't heard the truth from the elderly gentleman in Sidmouth. It was that I had heard the truth differently, put a different interpretation on it. For me, the Eagle of Abundance sounded like a symbol for everything that was fruitful and good — but that if misused needed the balancing power of the Eagle of Contrition. But maybe the Priest's truth was different.

"You are lied to," Father Wilhelm said, pointing at the lectern. "You call this Eagle of Abundance. It is not. It is Eagle of . . . how you say . . . avarice. It is bad. And the eagle you have is not contrition, it is vengeance. You go now and take the evil with you."

"Evil? I don't understand. They're just lumps of wood."

"No, not just wood," he said, letting go of my arm, and gesticulating to better express his words. "Separate, they are weak. Together . . .," he brought his hands together and made a sound like an explosion, his eyes wide and fearful.

"You mean, if the two come together they have destructive power?"

"*Ja*, that is correct. Now you must go," he said, taking hold of my arm again.

"But if that's true," I said, "Why don't we destroy them?"

Father Wilhelm shook his head, "No, not that. The power is contained in the symbol. If the symbol is destroyed, the power will be released. It is why we keep the eagle in our *Kapelle*. Hidden but under the watchful eye of Lord Jesus. You saw how I write, *nein*?"

"Yes, you were swapping your pen from one hand to the other."

"*Ja*. And why I do that?"

I shook my head.

"It is to keep balance in the world." He let go of me and raised his arms. "With the right hand I write the words of a vengeful God. With the left, I write for the Deceiver. Both need to be acknowledged. This satisfies them. If joined together, *unaufhaltsam*. How you say, unstoppable? You must return to England with your eagle. Keep it hidden. You are its custodian."

Suddenly, there was a loud crashing noise outside, accompanied by the screech of tearing and twisting metal. I ran from the chapel, through the courtyard and out of the gates. My hire car had been flattened into the gravel by a huge, driverless tractor that was careering out of control, destroying everything in its path.

The tractor came to a halt on top of the demolished outbuilding that had been clinging onto life in the vegetable garden. It left a silence that was terrifying. The only thing moving was the low cloud seeping over the mountains and into the forests. The Eagle of Vengeance had been destroyed.

I turned back to the gates but they had been closed. I tried to open them; they were locked. I shouted to be let back in, but my call was not answered. There was nothing I could do except set off walking back to Oppenau — an hour away on foot.

*   *   *

The walk gave me time to try and make sense of all that had happened but, no matter how I looked at it, it made no sense at all. By the time I reached the town I had explained it all away by telling myself that the mystery of the Eagles' provenance, and the evocative nature of the Black Forest landscape, had given credibility to the fanciful and totally fictitious tale conjured up by a fanatical monk in a remote monastery. I suddenly felt very foolish.

With my sensible head firmly back in place, I made a phone call to my travel insurers and was soon on my way to the nearest airport, Strasbourg. I had no wish to linger here any longer then needed.

*   *   *

The light was already fading as the 'plane reached cruising height. I gazed out of the aircraft window onto the clouds below, thinking only of getting home and putting all this nonsense behind me. I had been obsessed with this irrational mission for so long and neglected other, more important, issues. It was time to put things in order and get on with my life.

As I was making a mental note of all I had to do when I got home, a dark shadow moved across the sky. I blinked. Tired eyes see strange things. I looked again. There was no doubt — the darkening clouds were forming themselves into the shape of an eagle, wings outstretched, covering the whole sky. I shrunk back into my seat and pulled down the window blind. If I didn't look, it would go away. If I couldn't see, it didn't exist.

Suddenly, a familiar 'ping' noise sounded and the seat belt lights came on.

"We're expecting a little turbulence," said the calm voice of the Pilot over the tannoy system, "Please return to your seats and fasten your seatbelts."

The plane lurched and dropped. Passengers gasped. And then the engines roared as the 'plane climbed back to its cruising altitude.

With an increasing sense of dread, I slid the window blind back up. There was no mistaking the mighty head that was rearing up from the clouds, with its hooked yellow beak and cruel eyes. Turning its head in a final farewell, it dived towards the earth, flashing through the clouds like a lightning strike.

In that moment I knew that a great power had been unleashed and was bent on vengeance. I also knew there was nothing I, nor Father Wilhelm, could do to stop the horror that was about to descend upon the world.

Notes on
'Return of the Eagle'

The statue of the eagle that stands in Blackmore Gardens was bought by the chairman of the Sidmouth branch of the Royal British Legion who, in 2012, raised funds for it to be sited on a spot known locally as Lenin's Tomb. The plaque reads:

A
TRIBUTE TO
THE RESIDENTS
OF THE SID VALLEY
AND THE
SERVICE MEN AND WOMEN
WHO
TRAINED IN
ROYAL AIR FORCE
SIDMOUTH
DURING
THE SECOND WORLD WAR
1939 - 45

The story of how, and when, the Black Forest carving of an eagle was purchased from a Sidmouth antique shop, is true. It was purchased by the author in 1976 and is still in her possession. As far as she knows it does not have an evil counterpart and nor has it affected her life in any way — at least not as far as she knows . . .

If you've enjoyed this collection of short stories,

look out for more

Twisted Tales

written on the South West Coast Path

Twisted Tales of Cornwall

Twisted Tales of Somerset & North Devon

Twisted Tales of Dorset

As a self-published writer, the author needs, and encourages, reviews on Amazon and/or Goodreads. If you prefer, you can email your feedback via her website www.docdreamuk.com

AFTERWORD

The South Devon section of the South West Coast Path has stunning views, running as it does over the red cliffs that lead onto Torquay and from there onto the white cliffs of Beer. But sadly, when I walked this stretch in June 2017, all was not as expected.

It was never my intention to flag up problems in this series of books but the state of the path between Plymouth and Teignmouth is so bad in parts that it could well jeopardise the future of the path as a National walking trail.

There were a number of problems, including a lack of finger-posts, unmarked diversions around landslips, long diversions inland, skirting round private property or farmland, (Stoke Fleming comes to mind), paths that peter out to nothing and some that are so badly overgrown as to be barely passable. Add to that, misleading signage such as that at Brownstone Battery, two miles out of Kingswear, where there is a finger-post marked 'South West Coast Path To Brixham' that takes you down steep stone steps, right to the bottom of the cliff, only to take you all the way back up on a steep, narrow path, right back to where you started from! You can imagine with a tough, twelve mile day planned, this was not a welcome diversion. Even the coast guards in the look-out station could not find the 'real' path, which turned out to be signposted off a tarmac road a few hundred yards away in the opposite direction. Apart from the inconvenience of it all, parts of the path are dangerous because of a lack of maintenance — I still have the scars!

Add to that a proliferation of dog excrement in all the popular dog-walking areas, especially around Plymouth, and you will get an idea of how much this stretch of path needs to improve to keep its status as one of the most beautiful trails in England.

To find the path in such a bad state was all the more poignant when I passed a memorial bench, between Strete Gate and Strete, dedicated to Philip and Mary Carter — the couple who set up the path and got it adopted as a national trail. It will be a great shame if it is allowed to fall into disrepair after all their hard work.

In memory of

Philip and Mary Carter

Tireless campaigners for South West Coast Path
and founders of the South West Coast Path Association

Fortunately, things improved markedly on reaching the district of East Devon.

June 2017

About the Author

Jo is divorced with two grown up sons. She suffers from CWD, (Compulsive Writing Disorder), and has been scribbling down stories since she was knee high to a grasshopper. After too many careers, she decided to fulfil a lifelong ambition and go to University to study Science. On gaining a PhD in Chemistry, she secured a teaching position at the University of Nottingham and moved to a sleepy village in the East Midlands where she lived and worked in academia for over fifteen years. In 2011, after much soul searching, she finally departed the stage of 'normal' work in order to devote her life to writing.

Born and bred in Saddleworth, in the West Riding of Yorkshire, it wasn't long before the rugged Pennine landscape was calling her back home. She now lives in the village of Greenfield on the edge of the Dark Peak.

The author on the ferry from Salcombe to East Portlemouth.

Printed in Great Britain
by Amazon